Freddie Fernortner

Fearless First Grader ©

Darla Chipper Mr. Chewy

A Haunting We Will Go

BY JO

An AudioCraft Publishing, Inc. book

This book is a work of fiction. Names, places, characters and incidents are used fictitiously, or are products of the author's very active imagination.

Freddie Fernortner, Fearless First Grader®
#3: A Haunting We Will Go
ISBN 978-1-893699-81-6

Illustrations by Cartoon Studios, Battle Creek, Michigan

Visit www.freddiefernortner.com

Dickinson Press Inc., Grand Rapids MI, USA • Job 3924500 September 2011

A HAUNTING WE WILL GO

1

This is the story of how Freddie Fernortner and his two best friends, Darla and Chipper, along with Freddie's cat Mr. Chewy, discovered a haunted house. It's a very spooky story, too, so you might want to have some lights on while you read it.

One day, Chipper told Freddie and Darla about a haunted house that wasn't far from where they lived.

"My dad told me all about it," Chipper explained. "He said that it's only a short walk through the woods."

"Is it really haunted?" Darla asked.

"Yep," Chipper replied, nodding his head. "Dad says that it's been haunted for a long, long time."

"I'll bet it's scary!" Freddie said excitedly.

"That's what my dad said," Chipper piped. "Do you want to see if we can find it?"

Freddie didn't hesitate. "Yeah!" he exclaimed.

"I don't know," Darla said warily. Her eyes grew wide."There might be ghosts there."

"We won't go inside," Freddie said. "Let's just go and look. I'll bet it's really creepy looking."

Darla thought about it for a minute. "Well," she said, "I guess it would be okay to just *look* at it."

"It's right over there, through the forest," Chipper pointed. "Dad says it'll only take a few minutes to get there. He says there's even an old trail we can follow."

The three couldn't contain their excitement as they walked across the street, heading toward the deep, dark forest that was behind Chipper's house. Mr. Chewy followed, chewing a wad of gum and blowing bubbles. When the cat was only a small kitten, Freddie taught him how to chew gum and blow bubbles. That's how he got his name.

They walked around the house and found the old trail.

And they followed it.

Deep into the forest.

The thick branches above blocked out the sunlight, and the forest was very dark.

"This is spooky already," Darla said, as she looked around.

And Darla was right.

The forest *was* very spooky.

But things were about to get spookier.

2

The thick branches above grew thicker, and the forest became even darker.

"Gee," Chipper said. "I didn't realize that the forest was so dark."

"And this is the middle of the day," Freddie said.

"I sure wouldn't want to be in the forest at night," Darla said with a shudder.

The three continued walking along the path, looking warily around. They noticed different kinds of trees and shrubs.

"Look at that!" Freddie suddenly cried. He pointed toward the base of a tree only a few feet away. There, growing from the boggy ground, was a very large mushroom. It had a milky white stem, and a brown top covered with creamy spots.

"Wow!" Freddie said, as the three approached the mushroom. "I've never seen one so big in my whole life!"

Freddie, Chipper, and Darla crouched down to see the mushroom better. Mr. Chewy sat on the ground, chewing his gum.

"I'm going to touch it," Freddie said.

"Eeeewww!" Darla said with a grimace. "I bet it feels icky."

Freddie reached out and gently touched the soft top of the mushroom, being very careful so he didn't injure it.

"It's soft," he said, "and a little slimy."

Mr. Chewy sat up, walked over to the mushroom, and sniffed a few times.

Chipper reached out his hand and felt the mushroom. "You're right, Freddie," he said. "It *is* a little slimy."

"Gross!" Darla said.

"Touch it, Darla," Freddie said. "It won't bite you."

"I'm not going to touch it," Darla said, shaking her head.

"You big chicken," Chipper said.

"I'm not chicken," Darla said. "I just think it's icky. I don't want icky stuff on my fingers."

Freddie was about to stand up, when he noticed something near the mushroom.

"Holy cow!" he suddenly exclaimed.

He pointed.

Chipper looked.

Darla looked.

They gasped.

In the weeds, partially hidden, a pair of beady eyes glared back at them.

And, without warning, the creature attacked!

3

"Aaaaahhh!" Freddie screamed, and he fell backward.

"Oooooohhh!" Chipper cried, and he lost his balance and tumbled to the ground.

"Eeeeeek!" Darla shrieked. She, too, fell to the ground. Mr. Chewy jumped so fast he almost spit out his gum.

It didn't take long, however, for the three first graders and the cat to leap to their feet.

"It's a monster!" Chipper cried.

"It's a creature!" Darla exclaimed.

Freddie stood at a safe distance, looking at the thing that had suddenly leapt from its hiding place.

"It's . . . it's . . . it's only a toad!" he stammered. He took a step forward and knelt down. "Look at him!" he said. "That's the biggest toad I've ever seen!"

Chipper and Darla let out relieved sighs, and they walked up to Freddie and knelt down.

"You're right!" Chipper said. "That thing is gigantic!"

"Maybe that mushroom belongs to him," Darla said. "You know . . . so he has a place to go when it rains."

"It might be his chair," Chipper said. "I read somewhere that mushrooms are also called 'toadstools'."

"I'll bet you're right," Freddie said. "I'll bet the toad uses it as his chair."

Chipper reached out to touch the toad, but the toad wasn't going to have any part of it. It turned, and with one giant leap, bounded into the brush, and vanished.

"That was cool," Freddie said, standing up. "I wonder what else we'll find in the forest."

"I just want to find the haunted house," Chipper said. "I want to see a real, live ghost!"

"Ghosts aren't alive," Darla said. "That's why they're called 'ghosts'."

"I don't think there is such a thing as ghosts," Freddie said.

"Uh-huh," Darla said, nodding her head. "My cousin says that there is a ghost that lives in his basement. He says he feeds him marshmallows."

"Marshmallows?!?!" Chipper exclaimed. "That's the silliest thing I've ever heard! Ghosts don't eat marshmallows!"

"This ghost does," Darla insisted, bobbing her head. "And my cousin doesn't make things up."

Chipper shook his head. He'd never heard of a ghost that ate marshmallows.

Of course, he had no idea what ghosts ate, if they ate anything at all.

But he was sure that they didn't eat marshmallows.

"Come on," Freddie urged. "Let's keep going. The haunted house can't be far."

And Freddie was right. The three first graders didn't know it at the time, but they were only moments away from finding it.

The haunted house.

4

"Look!" Freddie gasped. He pointed.

Not far away, a dark, two-story home sat nestled tightly beneath large, old trees. The house was old, too, with broken windows and shutters that were falling off. Shingles had fallen from the roof.

"Wow," Darla breathed. "It's even creepier than I thought it would be."

3

"I wonder how long it's been here," Chipper said. "My dad said that it was here when he was a little boy. And my dad is super old."

The three continued to stare at the old house in the dark forest. Even Mr. Chewy seemed interested. He stopped chewing his gum and peered through the trees, gazing warily at the haunted house.

"Do you really think it's haunted?" Freddie asked.

"Sure," Chipper said. "That's what my dad says."

"Maybe your dad is just kidding," Darla said.

"Not about stuff like this," Chipper said. "If he says it's haunted, it's haunted."

"Let's go closer," Freddie urged.

"Do you think we should?" Darla asked. "I mean . . . if it's *really* haunted, maybe we shouldn't get too close."

"We won't go inside," Chipper said. "We'll just walk around outside."

"If we see any ghosts, I'm out of here," Darla said.

Freddie led the way along the trail, followed by Chipper, Darla, and Mr. Chewy. They walked slowly.

Freddie didn't admit it, but he *was* a bit frightened.

Chipper didn't say it, but he was a little scared, too.

So was Darla.

But, the three stuck together, relying on each other for support.

Freddie suddenly stopped walking, and Chipper bumped into him. Darla bumped into Chipper. Mr. Chewy was paying attention, however, and he stopped and sat on the trail before he bumped into anyone.

"Why did you stop?" asked Chipper.

Freddie didn't answer. Instead, he looked at the house that loomed through the trees.

"I just have a strange feeling, that's all," Freddie replied.

"Like what?" Darla asked.

"Like . . . like we're being watched," Freddie said. "Do you feel it?"

The three were silent for a moment. Then, Chipper spoke.

"Yeah," he replied quietly. "I feel it."

"I do, too," Darla said, looking around nervously.

They looked at the house.

Nothing there.

They looked to the left.

And saw nothing.

They looked to the right.

Nothing there.

They looked behind them.

Still nothing.

"Well, maybe we're just imagining things," Freddie said. "My mom says that I have a good imagination. Maybe nobody is watching us, after all."

Again, they looked at the old house.

Again, they looked to the left.

And to the right.

And behind them.

Nothing there.

But then, Darla looked up.

And screamed.

5

Darla's shriek echoed through the forest. It was so loud that it scared Chipper and Freddie.

They looked up—and saw what Darla was screaming about.

"That's cool!" Freddie exclaimed.

"That's awesome!" Chipper said.

Not far above the trio, on a low branch, was a raccoon.

Not a ghost.

Not a monster.

A raccoon.

When Darla screamed, it scared the poor critter. Quickly, the animal scrambled up to a higher branch.

"It's only a raccoon," Freddie said to Darla. "It's nothing to be afraid of."

"Yeah, but he surprised me," Darla said. "I thought it might be a scary monster."

"You were right, Freddie," Chipper said. "Something was watching us, after all."

They watched as the raccoon climbed higher and higher. Finally, it stopped and nestled on a branch high in the air. Mr. Chewy walked to the trunk of the tree and looked up. For a moment, the three first graders thought that he was going to climb the tree, but he didn't. He blew a bubble instead.

"Come on," Freddie said, and he started off again, heading for the house. Chipper and Darla followed.

In only a few seconds, they were standing near the old home, staring up at it.

"Gee," Freddie said. "It looks even scarier up close."

"Do you think anyone is home?" asked Darla.

"I don't think anyone's lived here for years," Chipper said. "It's falling apart. Nobody could live in a house like this."

"Ghosts can," said Darla.

Freddie shivered a teeny bit. Because the old house really did look like it was haunted.

"I don't see any ghosts," Chipper said.

"Maybe they're out back having a cookout," Freddie said with a laugh.

Darla snickered, and so did Chipper. The thought of ghosts sitting around a barbecue and grilling food *did* seem pretty funny.

The forest was very still. A few unseen birds chirped, but there were no other sounds.

"Let's walk around to the other side," Freddie said. He picked up Mr. Chewy.

The three clung tightly together as they made their way around to the back of the house. It was hard going, too, because the lawn was overgrown with tall weeds and bushes.

The back of the house was in worse shape than the front. All of the windows were broken out, and much of the siding had fallen away.

And one thing was for sure:

It *did* look like the house was haunted.

"Just think," Freddie said, gently stroking the cat in his arms. "There could be ghosts looking at us right now."

Darla shuddered. She didn't like the idea that a ghost might be spying on her.

"Did your dad say if he saw any ghosts?" Freddie asked.

"He didn't say," Chipper replied, shaking his head. "He just said that it's been haunted for a long time. Ever since he was a kid."

"I thought it would be scarier than this," Freddie said. "I mean . . . it looks scary, but not *that* scary. In fact, I'm not scared at all."

"Me neither," Chipper said.

"Same here," Darla agreed.

And that's when Freddie saw it.

A movement.

It wasn't a toad.

It wasn't a raccoon.

In fact, it wasn't an animal, at all.

Freddie, Darla, and Chipper were about to see a ghost.

6

It happened when they were just about ready to head home. Freddie handed Mr. Chewy to Chipper and was just about to take a step . . . but he didn't.

Because he saw something move.

Something inside the haunted house.

"What was that?" he said, pointing at a window on the second floor.

Chipper and Darla looked where Freddie was pointing.

"What was what?" Darla asked.

"Something moved up there," Freddie said. "I saw something move."

"Probably just another raccoon," Chipper said.

"No," Freddie said, shaking his head. "It was white. Like a sheet."

"You're just saying that to scare us," Darla said. "There's nothing up there."

"I'm telling you I saw something move up there," Freddie insisted. He kept staring at the broken window, waiting for whatever it was to move again.

Chipper stared, too.

And Darla stared.

Mr. Chewy blew a bubble and popped it. Gum flared out over his whiskers, and he licked it off.

"Are you *sure* you saw something move?" Chipper asked, placing Mr. Chewy on the ground.

Freddie nodded. “Yep,” he replied quietly. He pointed. “It was right up there.”

Birds in the trees stopped singing.

A gentle, mysterious breeze caused tree branches to tremble. A leaf fluttered past, caught in the light wind.

Freddie was silent.

Darla was silent.

Chipper was silent.

Mr. Chewy was silent.

And then—

A noise.

A noise could be heard coming from inside the house!

7

Freddie's knees knocked, and they sounded like this:

Clack-clack-clack-clack.

Darla's heart pounded, and it sounded like this:

Tha-thump, tha-thump, tha-thump, tha-thump.

Chipper gulped, and it sounded like this:

Gulp.

Mr. Chewy chomped his gum, and it sounded like this:

Chomp-chomp-chomp-chomp.

Inside the haunted house, they could hear a noise.

Footsteps.

Getting louder.

And louder.

Coming closer.

And closer . . .

"W-w-we've g-got t-to get out of h-here," Chipper stammered, "b-b-before th-th-th-that g-g-g-ghost g-g-gets us!"

But, they were so terrified that they couldn't move. They just stood there, frozen in fear, and these were the only sounds:

Clack-clack-clack-clack.

Tha-thump, tha-thump, tha-thump, tha-thump.

Gulp.

Chomp-chomp-chomp-chomp.

Suddenly, the noise inside the haunted house stopped.

A breeze blew softly.

Mr. Chewy stopped chewing and blew a bubble.

Slowly . . . very slowly . . . the front door of the haunted house slowly began to open.

And when they saw what had opened it, the three first graders screamed horrible, horrible screams.

Standing in the doorway was a ghost!

8

Freddie, Darla, Chipper, and Mr. Chewy were terrified.

In the doorway was the shape of a man.

But it couldn't be a man . . . because he was completely white!

"Let's get out of here!" Freddie shrieked, and without wasting a second more, the three, along with Mr. Chewy, turned and bolted across the yard. They reached the

trail that wound through the dark forest, and they kept running. They kept running, in fact, until they were all the way home, where they collapsed in the yard. Mr. Chewy sprawled out in the grass, too tired to chew his gum.

"I can't believe it!" Chipper gasped, trying to catch his breath. "My dad was right!"

"I didn't think ghosts were real," Freddie heaved. He, too, was trying to catch his breath.

"This has been the spookiest day of my life!" Darla said. She covered her eyes with her hands. "I can't believe we saw it! I can't believe we saw it!"

"We've got to tell someone!" Chipper said. "It might be a mean ghost, you know!"

"Those are the worst kind," Darla said with a nod.

"How would you know?" Chipper asked.

"Well, I think a mean ghost would be worse than a nice ghost," Darla replied.

"My mom will know what to do," Freddie said. He stood up. "Come on."

Darla and Chipper stood and followed Freddie across the yard and into the house. Mr. Chewy was too tired to move.

Freddie's mom was in the kitchen.

"Mom! You're not going to believe it!" Freddie exclaimed.

"Never in a million years!" Darla said.

"But we really saw it!" Chipper said.

Freddie's mom looked down and smiled. "Saw what?" she asked.

"A ghost!" Freddie cried.

"A mean ghost!" Darla piped.

Mrs. Fernortner smirked. "You guys," she said, shaking her head. "You know there is no such thing as ghosts."

"But we saw one, Mrs. Fernortner!" Chipper said. "Honest! We did!"

"It was in the haunted house in the forest!" Darla said. "He came to the front door!"

"He was all white, and really scary!" Freddie added.

"You three have good imaginations," Freddie's mom said. "You might have seen *something,* but I'm sure it wasn't a ghost."

"But it was, Mom!" Freddie said. "It really, really was!"

Nothing they said would change her mind. Mrs. Fernortner simply wouldn't believe that they had seen a ghost.

Later, the three were sitting on the porch, wondering what to do, trying to figure out how to get someone to believe them. They were silent for a long time.

Suddenly, Freddie's eyes lit up.

A smile grew on his face.

"What?" Chipper asked. "What are you thinking?"

"I've got it!" Freddie said. "Let's take a picture of the ghost! Then people would have to believe us!"

"That's a great idea!" Chipper said.

Darla's face blossomed with fear. "You mean . . . like . . . *with a camera?"* she stammered.

"Yeah!" Freddie replied. "I have one that Dad gave me! It's old, and it's not very good, but it works."

"But Freddie," Darla said, "that means that we have to go back to the haunted house."

"Yeah," Chipper said, scratching his head. "That's right. That might be kind of scary."

"All we have to do is get close enough to take a picture," Freddie said. "We'll knock on the door, and when the ghost comes, we'll take a picture and run away."

"I don't know," Chipper said. "I'm not sure if I want to see a ghost again."

"Same here," Darla said, crossing her arms.

"Think about it, you guys!" Freddie exclaimed. "If we can get a picture of a ghost, we'll be famous! We might even be in the newspaper!"

Suddenly, Chipper's mood changed. "The newspaper?!" he exclaimed. "That would be super-cool!"

Even Darla had to admit that she wouldn't mind being famous. "But I'm not going to be the one to knock on the door," she said.

"I'll knock on the door," Freddie said.

"Chipper, you can take the picture."

"What am *I* going to do?" Darla asked.

"You can run for help if the ghost eats us," Chipper said.

Darla's eyes just about popped right out of her head.

Chipper smiled. "Hey, I was only kidding," he said.

"There's nothing to worry about," Freddie said. "What could possibly go wrong?"

Lots. Lots could go wrong—

As Freddie, Darla, Chipper, and Mr. Chewy were about to find out.

9

Freddie went into his house and returned with a camera. It was silver and black, about the size of a candy bar, only thicker.

"There's one picture left on this roll of film," Freddie said. "This is going to be cool!"

"I hope you're right," Darla said.

"We're going to be famous!" Chipper said, and the three, followed by Mr. Chewy, headed back into the dark forest.

They stopped by the mushroom to see if the toad was around, but it wasn't.

"Maybe he's down by the lake having a couple of bugs with the guys," Chipper said.

They continued on.

The forest got darker.

They kept going.

It became even darker.

Soon, the house came into view. The three first graders stopped. Mr. Chewy stopped, blew a bubble, and popped it.

"There it is," Freddie said, his voice hushed. He handed the camera to Chipper.

"Uh, gee, Freddie," Chipper began. "I don't know. Maybe we shouldn't do this." Now that they'd actually arrived at the haunted house, Chipper wasn't sure he wanted to get any closer.

And he really didn't want to see the

ghost.

"It'll be fine," Freddie said.

Chipper was nervous. His hands trembled a tiny bit.

And we'll be famous, he thought. *If we get a picture of a real ghost, everyone in school will talk about us.*

Chipper took a deep breath. "Let's go," he said, as bravely as he could.

"You're not afraid?" Freddie asked Darla.

"Oh, I'm afraid, all right," Darla said. "But I'm just the lookout girl. If something happens to you guys, I'm going to run away faster than a duck chases a June bug."

Which is pretty fast, when you think about it.

Chipper scratched his head in confusion. "I didn't even know ducks liked June bugs," he said.

They walked slowly, taking soft steps, as they approached the house. Mr. Chewy followed, his wiry tail swishing slowly back and forth.

"See anything in the windows?" Chipper asked.

"Nope," Freddie replied. "Let's keep going."

They continued up to the haunted house, around back, through the tall grass. Soon, they saw the door where the ghost had appeared.

Suddenly, a loud noise came from inside the house!

Bang! Pound! Boom!

It was enough to almost make all three first graders jump out of their skin. Even Mr. Chewy was scared. His hair stood straight up, and he looked like a fuzzy balloon.

"He's here!" Freddie whispered hoarsely. *"He's still here!"* He handed the camera to Chipper.

"Okay," Freddie said. "Here's the plan: I'll run up and knock on the door. When the ghost comes, take a picture. As soon as you take the picture, yell something."

"What do you want me to yell?" Chipper asked.

"I don't care," Freddie said. "Anything. Just let me and Darla know that you've got the picture. Then, we run."

"Faster than a duck chasing a June bug," Darla peeped.

"Everybody ready?" asked Freddie.

Darla and Chipper nodded. Mr. Chewy blew a bubble.

Freddie drew a breath.

Here goes nothing, he thought.

Freddie walked slowly, carefully, to the front door.

He raised his fist.

He turned and looked at Chipper, Darla, and Mr. Chewy. Chipper was holding the camera up to his face. Darla covered her eyes with her hands, but she was peeking just a tiny bit.

Freddie turned back around and faced the door.

He paused one last time.

Then—

He pounded four times on the heavy wood door.

Boom! Boom! Boom! Boom!

Then, just as quickly as he had pounded, he spun on his heels and darted off, not stopping until he reached his friends.

They waited nervously.

Nothing happened.

They waited some more.

Until—

A noise.

From somewhere inside the haunted house came a noise.

A noise that sounded like footsteps.

A noise that was getting louder.

Coming closer . . .

"Get ready," Freddie whispered to Chipper.

"I'm shaking so bad that I can't hold the camera still," Chipper whispered back.

"I can't bear to look," Darla said. Her hands were still covering her eyes.

And then—

The front door opened, and the ghostly-white figure appeared.

There was a soft *click* as Chipper took the picture.

"Got it!" he yelled, just like Freddie had told him to do.

"Run!" Freddie said, and they tore through the long grass faster than ducks chasing June bugs. They didn't even slow down until they were halfway through the forest.

Then, and only then, did they realize that Darla wasn't with them . . .

10

Freddie and Chipper gasped in horror. Mr. Chewy was there, but Darla was nowhere to be seen.

"Darla!" Freddie called. "Darla, where are you?"

They waited.

Darla didn't appear.

"We have to go back for her," Freddie said.

"What if the ghost got her?" Chipper

said.

"What if—"

Suddenly, they heard Darla's voice in the distance!

"Thanks for waiting!" she shouted angrily. "That ghost could have got me, and you guys wouldn't have even cared!"

Then, they could see her coming toward them on the trail. There were dark stains on her jeans, especially around her knees.

Freddie and Chipper ran back to her.

"What happened?" Freddie asked.

"I fell, that's what happened," Darla snapped. "I tripped on a root back there."

"Why didn't you yell?" Chipper said.

"Because I landed on my tummy and knocked the wind out of me," Darla said. "I could hardly breathe!"

"Are you hurt?" Freddie asked.

Darla shook her head. "No, but my mom is going to have a cow when she sees how dirty my pants are!"

The three started walking, quickly, making their way out of the dark forest.

"I can't wait until we get the film developed!" Freddie said. "Then we'll have a real picture of a ghost, and everyone will *have* to believe us!"

"And we'll be famous!" Chipper said. "I want to be in the newspaper!"

Four days later, Freddie called Chipper and Darla on the telephone and told them that the film was ready. His dad was going to stop by the store, pick up the pictures, and bring them home with him after work. At five fifteen (that was about the time that Freddie's father normally returned from work) the three first graders and Mr. Chewy gathered in Freddie's yard to wait for his dad.

After a few minutes, they saw Mr. Fernortner's minivan coming up the street.

Would the picture turn out? Would it actually show the ghost that haunts the old house deep in the dark forest?

They were about to find out.

11

Freddie, Chipper, and Darla stood waiting anxiously at the edge of the driveway. Freddie had given Mr. Chewy a new stick of gum, and the cat was sitting near a tree, blowing bubbles one after another.

The minivan pulled up, and Mr. Fernortner got out. He was carrying his black briefcase.

And an envelope.

"I know what you guys are looking

for," he said, holding out the envelope.

Freddie could hardly contain his excitement as he took the envelope from his father.

"Thanks, Dad!" Freddie said.

"Yeah, thanks, Mr. Fernortner!" Chipper and Darla said.

"No problem," Mr. Fernortner replied, and he walked into the house.

Freddie ripped open the envelope and began thumbing through the pictures. Chipper and Darla peered over his shoulder.

"Not that one," Freddie was saying. "No, not that one or that one."

And then—

There it was.

The picture of the ghost.

It was blurry, but it clearly showed the white form, standing in the doorway.

"We got it!" Freddie said, jumping up and down. "A picture of a real ghost!"

Darla frowned. "But it's fuzzy," she said. "It's hard to see what it is."

"That's because I was shaking so hard," Chipper said. "I couldn't hold the camera still."

"But we still got it!" Freddie said. "I told you it would work! I told you!"

"We're going to be famous!" Chipper said. "I just know it!"

"We've got to take it to show-and-tell tomorrow," Freddie said. "Everyone in class is going to freak out!"

"Everyone is going to think we're so cool!" Darla said.

But that's not what happened. What happened was exactly the opposite.

Freddie, Chipper, and Darla were in for a big surprise . . .

12

"And who would like to go next for show-and-tell?" Mrs. Beanswiggle asked. Mrs. Beanswiggle was room twenty-seven's teacher—Freddie's room—and he liked her very much. She was very nice, and they did a lot of fun things in class.

Like show-and-tell.

Freddie waved frantically. "We'd like to go next, Mrs. Beanswiggle," he said excitedly.

"All right, Freddie," his teacher said. "Come to the front of the class."

In his hand, Freddie held the picture. He stood and walked to the front of the room. Chipper and Darla followed.

"Three of you?" Mrs. Beanswiggle said.

"Well, we were all together when we did this," Freddie explained.

"I see," said Mrs. Beanswiggle. "And just what did you do?"

"Well, not far from where we live, there's a haunted house," replied Chipper.

The students gasped.

"We saw a ghost!" Darla blurted.

The students gasped louder.

"And we took a picture of it!" Chipper said proudly.

The students gasped even louder.

Without saying anything more,

Freddie held up the picture.

The students looked on. Some of them frowned. Others had confused looks on their faces.

"That's not a ghost," one boy said. "That just looks like a big blurry pillow or something."

"Yeah," said another student. "That

doesn't look like a ghost at all."

"No, really," Freddie said. "It's a ghost. All three of us saw it, didn't we?"

Chipper and Darla nodded.

"Yeah, we were there," Darla said.

"I took the picture," Chipper said proudly. "It's a little blurry because I was shaking and couldn't hold the camera still."

"It was really scary," Freddie said.

"That's very nice, Freddie," Mrs. Beanswiggle said. "But, are you sure it's a ghost?"

"Yes, we're sure," Freddie said. "It's probably still there."

While no one was looking, a boy in the second row had taken off his shoe and his sock. He placed the white sock over his hand and held it up.

"Hey Freddie!" he said, moving his hand beneath the sock. The sock came alive, looking like a white hand puppet. "Look Freddie!" he said. "I'm a ghost! Boo! Boo! Boo!"

Students began laughing.

"Maxwell!" Mrs. Beanswiggle scolded. "Put that sock back on this instant! And your shoe!"

Several students were still giggling and snickering.

"It's a real ghost, Mrs. Beanswiggle," Freddie said. He turned and faced his classmates. "Really," he said, still holding the picture up for all to see. "It's a real ghost."

"Take your seats," Mrs. Beanswiggle said to the trio at the front of the class.

Freddie, Darla, and Chipper looked hurt and sad as they took their seats. They thought that their classmates would be excited. Instead, they poked fun at them.

Later, during recess, Freddie, Darla and Chipper met on the playground at the teeter-totter.

"There's only one thing we can do," Freddie said. "If we want people to believe us, we're going to have to go back and take another picture."

"No way," Darla said, shaking her head. Her dark hair slapped her cheeks. "I've been there enough. I don't want to go back."

"Me neither," Chipper said.

"But guys . . . if we can take a better picture, then people will believe us. The only reason they don't believe us right now is because the picture is blurry. We know what we saw, because we were there. We have to get a better picture."

"Fine," Chipper said. "But you can count me out."

"Me too," Darla said. "That ghost gave me the heebie-jeebies." She shivered.

"What's a heebie-jeebie?" Chipper asked. He scratched his head.

Darla looked confused. "Well," she said, "I guess I really don't know what they are. But when I saw the ghost, I got them."

So, Freddie made his mind up then and there.

He *would* go back to the haunted house.

He *would* take another picture of the ghost.

That very day, right after school.

Alone.

The thought spooked him. He didn't want to go to the haunted house alone, but he couldn't force his friends to go with him. Mr. Chewy would, of course, go with him . . . but the cat was probably more afraid of the ghost than he was.

I'll just knock on the door and take the picture myself, he thought. *Everything will be fine.*

As it turned out, everything wasn't going to be fine.

Not at all.

13

When Freddie arrived home, Mr. Chewy was waiting for him on the porch, just like he always did.

"Well, buddy," Freddie said, as he reached down to pet the cat. "We're going back to the haunted house today. Just me and you."

The cat blew a big bubble. It popped with a sharp *snap!*

Freddie went inside. His mother was

seated at the dining room table. She was holding a pair of scissors, clipping coupons from a newspaper.

"Hi, Mom," Freddie said, as he dropped his backpack on a chair.

"Hi, Freddie," his mother said. "How was school?"

"Oh, okay," Freddie said. "We took the picture of the ghost to school, but nobody believed us."

"Oh?" his mother said.

"Yeah, but the picture is blurry because Chipper was shaking so much. I'm going to go back and take another picture today."

"As long as you stay out of the house," his mother warned.

"Oh, I'm not going to go inside. I'm just going to wait for the ghost to come to the door, take a picture, and run."

Freddie found his camera in his bedroom. He carried it outside, where Mr. Chewy still sat on the porch, chewing gum and blowing bubbles.

But there were two people standing in the yard.

Two kids.

Not just kids . . . but first graders.

Chipper and Darla.

"We thought about it," Chipper said. "We just couldn't let you go back to the haunted house alone."

"So we're going with you," Darla said.

Freddie smiled. "Thanks, guys," he said.

So, the three started off into the woods, followed by Mr. Chewy. They passed the large mushroom again and looked for the big toad, but it wasn't anywhere in sight.

And the forest grew dark.

Darker.

And darker.

Soon, the haunted house came into view.

14

"Everybody ready?" Freddie asked.

"I am," Chipper said.

"Me, too, I guess," Darla said.

"Let's go," Freddie said, and they made their way through the tall grass and around the other side of the house.

"This time, I'll knock," Chipper said bravely. "You take the picture, Freddie. Maybe you won't shake as much as I did."

Freddie and Darla stayed back from

the porch as Chipper walked up to the door.

He raised his fist and gave three quick, hard raps.

Knock-knock-knock.

Then he spun, darted from the porch, and ran to where Freddie and Darla waited.

Inside the haunted house, they heard a noise.

Freddie held his camera up, peering through the viewfinder. He was ready.

Inside the house, the noise was getting closer.

And closer.

The ghost was coming.

The door opened slowly . . .

Slowly . . .

And there stood a man.

Not a scary ghost, but a normal man, wearing blue overalls and a red shirt. He was holding a hammer.

"Can I help you?" the man asked.

Freddie lowered the camera. "Um, yeah," he said. "We were looking for the ghost."

"Ghost?" the man asked. "Where?"

"Here," Chipper said. "In this house. He was here a few days ago. We even took a picture of him."

The man looked puzzled. "Ghost?" he said. "There's no ghost around here."

"But there is," Darla insisted. "We have a picture to prove it."

"We were here a few days ago," Freddie explained. "A ghost came to the door, and we took a picture."

The man still looked confused.

Then, he smiled.

"This 'ghost'," he began. "Was he about my size?"

Freddie, Chipper and Darla looked him up and down. They agreed that the ghost was about the same size as the man.

"Was he all white?" the man asked. "Even his face and hair?"

"Yeah!" Freddie exclaimed. "You've seen him?"

"You might say that," the man replied. "You see, I am the ghost."

"But . . . but you're . . . you're just a guy," Darla said.

"Yes, but let me explain. I've been working to fix this old house up. A few days ago, I was working with drywall."

"What's 'drywall'?" Darla asked.

"Well, it's kind of like big sheets, like thick, white paneling." The man spread his arms wide. "It's used for walls and ceilings. But it's all white, and can be very, very messy. When you work with it, the white dust can go everywhere."

"You . . . you mean that you were covered with drywall dust?" Freddie asked.

"That's right," the man said. "I was the one who came to the door when you knocked."

"So, there's no ghost here?" Darla asked. She sounded relieved.

The man shook his head. "I'm afraid not," the man said. "Just me. Sorry to disappoint you."

And so, the mystery of the haunted house was solved. There was no ghost there, after all. Just a man who was working inside to fix up the old home. A man covered with white drywall dust.

"Well, it sure was fun, anyway," Freddie said, as the three headed back through the forest. "Even if the house isn't really haunted, it was still a cool adventure."

They stopped near the mushroom. The toad was there, sitting near a tree!

"Hey, there he is!" Chipper cried. "The giant toad is back!"

"Don't get too close," Freddie said. "We don't want to scare him."

But Mr. Chewy wasn't listening. The cat had spotted the toad and was very curious. He walked up to the creature and sniffed.

The toad didn't do anything. It just sat there, ignoring Mr. Chewy.

Mr. Chewy sniffed again.

Then, he licked the toad!

Suddenly, the cat jumped back, shaking his head rapidly, and spitting. He sputtered so hard that he spit out his gum.

The toad just sat there, looking mad.

Freddie, Chipper, and Darla burst out laughing.

"That'll teach Mr. Chewy not to lick any more toads," Freddic said with a chuckle.

They left the toad and the mushroom and walked home.

"Well, what are we going to do this weekend?" Chipper asked. It was Friday, and that meant they didn't have to go back to school for two whole days.

"Yeah," Darla said merrily. "Let's do something really fun."

"Let's do something to make some money," Freddie suggested.

They sat on the porch, thinking. Mr. Chewy sat in the grass, waiting for Freddie to give him another stick of gum.

"We could have a lemonade stand," Chipper suggested. "That might make us some money."

"Yeah, but not many people come by

our street," Freddie said. "We wouldn't have very many customers."

Just then, a lady and her dog hustled by on the sidewalk. The dog was big, and the lady was having a hard time holding on to the leash. She noticed the three first graders on the porch.

"Sometimes, I don't know if I'm walking him or if he's walking me," she said, huffing and puffing. The dog continued pulling, and the lady held the leash and bustled away.

"That's it!" Freddie cried. "I know what we can do to make some money!"

"What?" Chipper asked.

"Yeah, what?" echoed Darla.

"It'll be great!" exclaimed Freddie.

"What will be great?" Chipper and Darla asked.

"Meet me here on my porch at eight

o'clock tomorrow morning," Freddie said. "You'll see! I've got a great idea!"

NEXT:
FREDDIE FERNORTNER, FEARLESS FIRST GRADER

BOOK FOUR:

FREDDIE'S DOG WALKING SERVICE

CONTINUE ON TO READ THE FIRST CHAPTER FOR FREE!

1

Freddie Fernortner squinted in the sun. His friend, Darla, and his other friend, Chipper, stood next to him. They were his best friends in the whole world. Once, they had built a flying bicycle together. It really worked, too. Then, there was the time that they hunted for super-scary night thingys in Freddie's back yard.

The point is, they did a lot of things together . . . because that's what best friends do.

Mr. Chewy, Freddie's cat that chews bubble gum, was laying in the grass nearby. Mr. Chewy was also one of Freddie's best friends.

It was Saturday morning. Just yesterday, the three had been sitting in the very same spot, thinking of what they could do for fun over the weekend. Freddie suggested that they do something to make money. He had a great idea, but he wasn't going to tell Darla and Chipper until that very day.

"Okay," Chipper said to Freddie that Saturday morning. "What's your big idea?"

"Right here," Freddie replied, digging into his pocket. He pulled out a wad of papers. Each piece of paper was small, about the size of a candy wrapper.

He handed one to Darla, and one to Chipper.

Chipper looked at the paper and the handwriting on it. Then, he began reading out loud.

"Freddie's Dog Walking Service," he said.

Darla read the next line. "No pooch too big, no pup too small."

"A dog walking service?" Chipper asked.

"That's right," Freddie said with a wide grin. "Remember that lady we saw yesterday?"

Darla and Chipper nodded. They had watched a lady struggling to walk her big, strong dog.

"Well," Freddie continued, "she said that sometimes she needs help walking her dog. I'll bet there are a lot of people that need that sort of help."

"But how are we going to make money doing that?" Darla asked.

"Simple," Freddie said. "We'll go around the block, knock on doors, and ask people if they need someone to walk their dog. We charge twenty-five cents for each dog."

"But your paper says *Freddie's* Dog Walking Service," Chipper said. "What are Darla and I going to do?"

"You'll be my helpers," Freddie said proudly, "and we'll split all of the money evenly, so we all make the same amount."

"That sounds fair," Darla said.

"Sounds easy," Chipper said. "And besides . . . I like dogs. It'll be a lot of fun."

Chipper was right: they were going to have a lot of fun. Gobs of fun, in fact.

Little did they know that Freddie's Dog Walking Service was about to turn the neighborhood upside down.

DON'T MISS FREDDIE FERNORTNER, FEARLESS FIRST GRADER BOOK 4: FREDDIE'S DOG WALKING SERVICE

Don't miss these exciting, action-packed books by Johnathan Rand:

Michigan Chillers *(reading age 7-13)*

#1: Mayhem on Mackinac Island
#2: Terror Stalks Traverse City
#3: Poltergeists of Petoskey
#4: Aliens Attack Alpena
#5: Gargoyles of Gaylord
#6: Strange Spirits of St. Ignace
#7: Kreepy Klowns of Kalamazoo
#8: Dinosaurs Destroy Detroit
#9: Sinister Spiders of Saginaw
#10: Mackinaw City Mummies

American Chillers: *(reading age 7-13)*

#1: The Michigan Mega-Monsters
#2: Ogres of Ohio
#3: Florida Fog Phantoms
#4: New York Ninjas
#5: Terrible Tractors of Texas
#6: Invisible Iguanas of Illinois
#7: Wisconsin Werewolves
#8: Minnesota Mall Mannequins
#9: Iron Insects Invade Indiana
#10: Missouri Madhouse
#11: Poisonous Pythons Paralyze Pennsylvania
#12: Dangerous Dolls of Delaware
#13: Virtual Vampires of Vermont
#14: Creepy Condors of California
#15: Nebraska Nightcrawlers
#16: Alien Androids Assault Arizona
#17: South Carolina Sea Creatures

Adventure Club series: *(reading age 7-13)*

#1: Ghost in the Graveyard
#2: Ghost in the Grand

www.americanchillers.com

AudioCraft Publishing, Inc.
PO Box 281
Topinabee Island, MI 49791

WATCH FOR MORE *FREDDIE FERNORTNER, FEARLESS FIRST GRADER* BOOKS, COMING SOON!